Tiger Toothache

by Patricia M. Stockland
illustrated by Ryan Haugen

visit us at
www.abdopublishing.com

Published by Magic Wagon, a division of the ABDO Publishing Group, 8000 West 78th Street, Edina, Minnesota, 55439. Copyright © 2008 by Abdo Consulting Group, Inc. International copyrights reserved in all countries. All rights reserved. No part of this book may be reproduced in any form without written permission from the publisher.
Looking Glass Library™ is a trademark and logo of Magic Wagon.

Printed in the United States.

Text by Patricia M. Stockland
Illustrations by Ryan Haugen
Edited by Nadia Higgins
Interior layout and design by Becky Daum
Cover design by Becky Daum

Library of Congress Cataloging-in-Publication Data
Stockland, Patricia M.
  Tiger toothache / Patricia M. Stockland ; illustrated by Ryan Haugen.
     p. cm. — (Safari friends—Milo & Eddie)
  ISBN 978-1-60270-087-1
  [1. Elephants—Fiction. 2. Monkeys—Fiction. 3. Tigers—Fiction. 4. Hippopotamus—Fiction. 5. Dental care—Fiction. 6. Grasslands—Fiction. 7. Africa—Fiction.] I. Haugen, Ryan, 1972- ill. II. Title.
PZ7.S865Tig 2008
[E]—dc22
                                                            2007036996

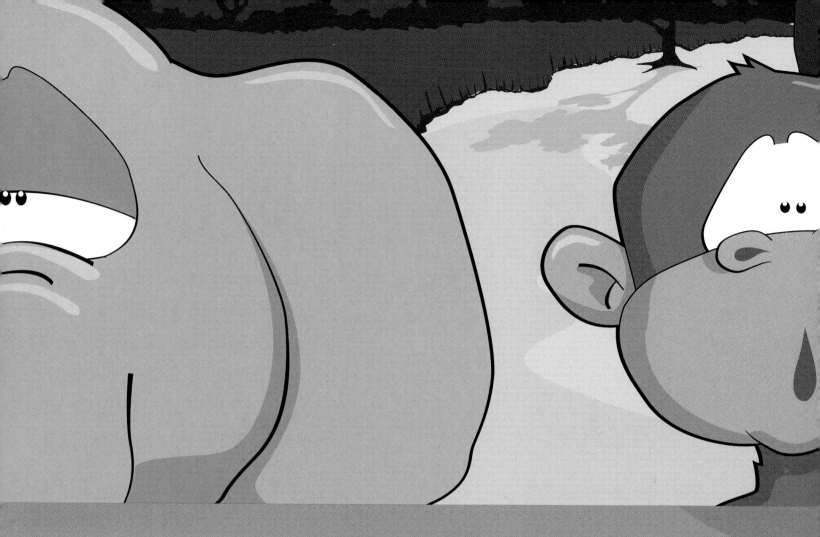

"Roar! . . . Rooaa*arrr!* . . . *Roooaaarrrr!*"

Milo the monkey almost jumped out of his fur.

"Did you hear that?" he squeaked to his friend, Eddie the elephant. But Eddie didn't answer.

"Eddie!" Milo shouted.

"Huh?" Eddie said, rubbing his eyes.

"Did you hear that?" Milo said.

"Hear what?" Eddie said.

Eddie and Milo were camping in the savanna grasses. It was very, very late at night.

"That growly, howly noise," replied Milo. He peeked up from his hammock and peered across the grass.

"Why, I think I did hear something, now that you mention it," said Eddie. Of course, Eddie hadn't heard much of anything over the snores from his trunk.

"What could it be, Eddie? A hungry tiger? Or a bear? Or a monkey-eating mongoose?" Milo hissed. "Eddie, we can't just sit here like two big bowls of wildebeest food. We have to find out!"

Eddie climbed out of his hammock. He usually didn't wander around at this time of night. But he sensed Milo was scared, and he wanted to be a good friend.

"OK, you stay here. I'll go," said Eddie. "Which way do you think the sound came from?"

"Over by that termite mound, I'm fairly certain," whispered Milo.

Eddie wandered off through the darkness. He was almost at the termite mound when—

"*Roooaaarrr!*"

"Yeeeeeooow!" Eddie yelped. He shot up like a circus elephant on a trampoline.

"*Rooooaaarrr!*" This time it sounded like the *roar* was coming from his own belly.

Eddie looked down. There was one of his old friends.

"Why, hello there!" he said. "Why are you yelling?"

Tasha the tiger lay at Eddie's feet, rolling and wriggling and squirming about.

"Hey, Milo! It's just Tasha! Come fast! I think she might be hurt!" Eddie called.

Milo bounded over. "What's the problem?" he asked.

"It's my *tooth!*" Tasha exclaimed. "I have a terrible, terrible toothache. I can't sleep, I can't eat—I can't even chase termites!"

"That's horrendous and horrible!" said Eddie. "What can we do to help?"

"Well, do you know any dentists?" asked Tasha.

"As a matter of fact, we do," said Milo. "Follow us!"

The trio took off through the great, great grasslands. They tromped and they stomped and they marched right along. All the while, Eddie told a story about how he once chipped a tusk on a teacup. Tasha listened politely. Milo listened politely. And before they knew it, the sun woke up.

"Here we are," announced Milo, stopping quickly. Eddie was not ready for the quick stop, and the three travelers landed in a pile.

"*Roooaaarrr!* . . . Oh, my tooth!" yelled Tasha.

"What and who in the world is waking me up?" thundered a voice from the riverbank.

"It's just us, Henrietta," hollered Milo.

"By golly, hello there!" boomed the hippopotamus in the mud. "I thought someone was waking me up for emergency dental work, but I see you're just here early for tea. I'll put on a pot and get you a spot to eat." With that, the hippo headed into the water.

"Wait, Henrietta! We do need some help," explained Milo. "Our friend Tasha the tiger has a terrible, terrible, horrendous, horrible toothache."

"Hmmmmm," the hippo said as she wandered up the bank. "I see, I see." She put on her glasses. "Let's just have a look, and then we can see what the bother is."

Eddie and Milo just shrugged at each other. Tasha already had her mouth wide open.

"Oh, *my!*" exclaimed Henrietta. "What a beautiful, big set of teeth you have!" That reminded Henrietta of her own beautiful teeth. The hippo pulled out a hand mirror to admire her pearly whites.

"If you wouldn't mind," said Tasha, "I could really use some help. Perhaps if you could just . . ."

"Oh, yes, I'm so sorry. Silly me," said Henrietta. She handed her mirror to Milo and began to poke around in Tasha's teeth. The hippo first inspected the gums, then the molars, then the roof of Tasha's mouth. She stretched the tiger's cheeks this way and that.

"Eddie, do you happen to have a toothpick handy?" asked Henrietta.

"Absolutely," said Eddie. "I always keep some around for cleaning my tusks." He handed Henrietta a toothpick.

"Aha!" Henrietta said. "I've found it!" Henrietta pulled out a crumbly-munchy kind of thing from Tasha's teeth.

The others looked at it. "What is that? A coconut hair dumpling?" Milo guessed. "Or perhaps a rattlesnake skin popover?" Eddie suggested.

"It's a piece of popcorn!" Henrietta declared.

Tasha breathed a tremendous sigh of relief. "Thank you so much," she purred.

"Don't be too relieved," said Henrietta with her hands on her hippo hips. "That could have become a cavity. Haven't you been flossing? Haven't you been brushing?"

Eddie and Milo looked at Tasha. The tiger was blushing.

"Well . . .," she stammered. "I guess I haven't, really, because, I, um . . ."

"No excuses! Here, take this. And this! And take better care of your teeth!" said Henrietta. She handed the tiger some zebra-tail floss and a wild boar bristle toothbrush.

"Why, thank you! Thank you so much!" exclaimed Tasha. "To be entirely honest, I've never had a real toothbrush before."

"Well then, it's about time," said Henrietta. "I brush every morning and every night, and just look at the wonders it's done for me!"

And with that, the hippo gave Eddie, Milo, and Tasha a great big, beautiful toothy grin.

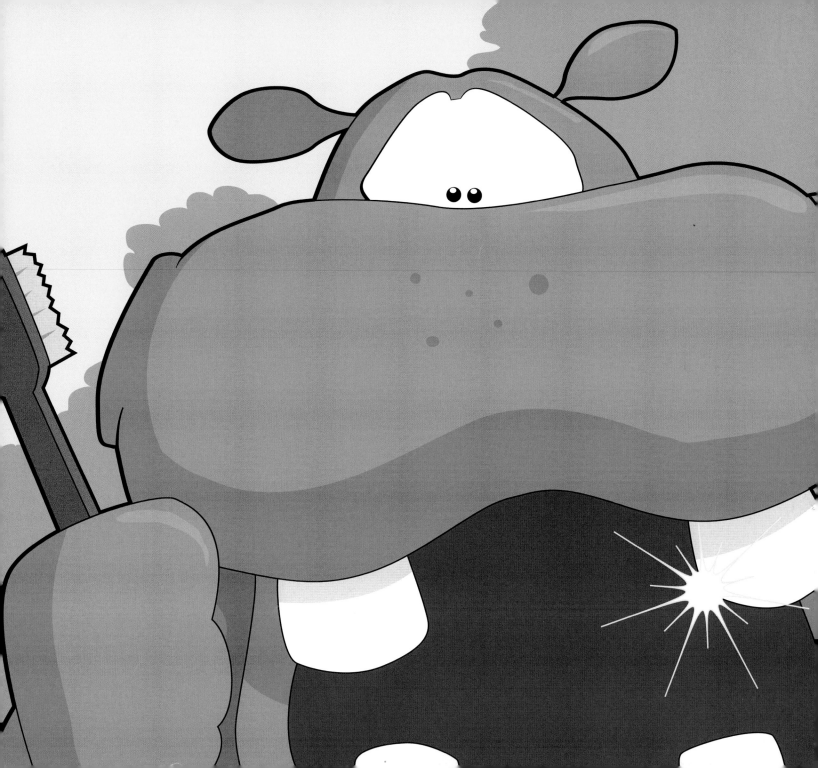

Savanna Facts

A tiger usually has 30 teeth. Its pointy canine teeth are bigger than the teeth of any other member of the cat family.

A hippopotamus's canine teeth can be as long as 20 inches (51 cm)!

Dentists recommend that you brush at least twice a day. Flossing between your teeth is also important for healthy gums. And don't forget to brush your tongue!